STORYBOOK AND CD

This is the story of Mowgli's adventures in the jungle. You can read along with me in your book. Let's begin now.

For more information address Disney Press,
1101 Flower Street, Glendale, California 91201

Printed in the United States of America
First Edition
1 3 5 7 9 10 8 6 4 2
ISBN 978-1-4847-0091-4
G942-9090-6-13281

For more Disney Press fun, visit www.disneybooks.com

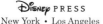
DISNEP PRESS
New York • Los Angeles

SUSTAINABLE FORESTRY INITIATIVE

Certified Chain of Custody
At Least 20% Certified Forest Content
www.sfiprogram.org
SFI-00993

For Text Only

Many strange legends are told of the jungles of far-off India. They speak of Bagheera the black panther, and of Baloo the bear. They tell of Kaa the sly python, and of the lord of the jungle, the great tiger Shere Khan. But of all these legends, none is so strange as the story of a small boy named Mowgli.

Mowgli, you see, had been left all alone in the jungle as a baby. He was found by Bagheera the panther. Bagheera could not give the small, helpless Man-cub care and nourishment, so he took the boy to the den of a wolf family with young cubs of their own. And that is how it happened that Mowgli, as the Man-cub came to be called, was raised among the wolves.

Ten times the rains came and went, and still Mowgli lived with the wolves. The Man-cub loved his pack and thought of the wolves as his brothers. Then, one day, everything changed. The tiger Shere Khan had returned to the jungle.

Akela, the leader of the pack, gathered the wolves at Council Rock.

"The Man-cub can no longer stay with the pack," he said. "The strength of the pack is no match for the tiger."

Out of the shadows stepped Bagheera the panther. "Perhaps I can be of help," he said. "I know a Man-village where he'll be safe. Mowgli and I have taken many walks into the jungle together. I'm sure he'll go with me."

So it was decided. Bagheera would take the Man-cub to safety.

When the greenish light of the
jungle morning slipped through the leaves,
Bagheera and Mowgli set out. All day they
walked, and when night fell, they slept on a
high branch of a giant banyan tree. All this
seemed like an adventure to Mowgli. But when
he learned that he was to leave the jungle, he
was horrified.

"No!" cried Mowgli. "I want to stay in the
jungle. I'm not afraid. I can look after myself."

And so, as Bagheera slept, Mowgli slipped
down a length of trailing vine and ran away.

Mowgli had not gone far when he saw a baby elephant march past him. "Hello. What are you doing?" Mowgli asked.

The baby elephant explained that he and the other elephants were doing drills.

"Can I do it, too?" Mowgli asked.

"Sure. Just do what I do," the baby answered. "But don't talk in ranks. It's against regulation."

All day, Mowgli marched beside the baby elephant. He was very happy to have found a new family in the jungle.

But when Colonel Hathi, the proud leader of the elephant herd, found Mowgli, he was very angry.

"A Man-cub. Oh, this is treason. Sabotage!" Hathi cried. "I'll have no Man-cub in my jungle!"

At that moment, Bagheera appeared. He had been searching for Mowgli all day.

"I can explain," the panther told Colonel Hathi. "The Man-cub is with me. I'm taking him back to the Man-village."

Colonel Hathi nodded. "Very well. Carry on," he said.

Mowgli and Bagheera had not gone far when the
Man-cub asked, "Bagheera, where are we going?"

"You're going back to the Man-village right now!" the
panther answered.

But Mowgli still did not want to leave the jungle. "I'm
staying right here," he said, grabbing hold of a small tree.

Bagheera grabbed Mowgli's pants between his teeth and began to pull. "You're going if I have to drag you every step of the way!" he said.

But still Mowgli refused.

Finally, Bagheera had had enough. "That does it," he cried. "From now on, you're on your own. Alone!" And with that, the panther stormed off, leaving Mowgli all by himself.

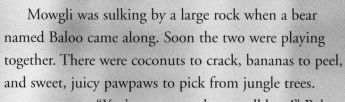

Mowgli was sulking by a large rock when a bear named Baloo came along. Soon the two were playing together. There were coconuts to crack, bananas to peel, and sweet, juicy pawpaws to pick from jungle trees.

"You're gonna make a swell bear!" Baloo told Mowgli.

Mowgli was having such fun in the jungle! Now he really didn't want to leave!

But the jungle was dangerous.
Sly old Kaa the python would
have loved to squeeze Mowgli
tight in his coils.

Even worse, Shere Khan the
tiger had learned that there was
a Man-cub in the jungle. And he
was determined to find him.

There were other dangers, too.
One day, Baloo and Mowgli were
enjoying a dip in a jungle river when
down swooped the monkey folk.
Before Baloo knew what was happening,
the monkeys had snatched up the Man-cub.
They tossed him through the air from
hand to hand and swung away with
him through the trees.

Off in the jungle, Bagheera heard Mowgli's cry.

"They ambushed me," Baloo told Bagheera. "Thousands of 'em. I jabbed with my left, and then I swung with a right, and then . . ." Baloo trailed off.

"For the last time, what happened to Mowgli?" Bagheera asked.

"Them monkeys carried him off!" gasped Baloo.

Bagheera raced away at once. He had to rescue Mowgli!

Bagheera and Baloo raced to the ruined city where the monkeys made their home. They found Mowgli a prisoner of Louie, king of the apes.

"What I desire is Man's red fire," King Louie told Mowgli. "Now give me the secret so I can be like you."

But before Mowgli could answer, Baloo and Bagheera whisked him away.

   "Look, Mowgli," Baloo said when they were safe.
"I got to take you back to the Man-village."
   "But you said we were partners," Mowgli said.
   Baloo tried to explain, but Mowgli would not listen.
Angry, he ran away. And that was when Shere Khan found
him at last.

When Mowgli caught sight of the tiger, Shere Khan asked, "Well, Man-cub, aren't you going to run?"

But Mowgli did not have the wisdom to be afraid. "Why should I run?" he asked, staring at Shere Khan as the tiger gathered himself to pounce. "You don't scare me."

With a mighty roar, Shere Khan lunged at Mowgli. He would teach the boy to be afraid of him.

Suddenly, there was a flash of lightning. A dead tree nearby caught fire.

Mowgli snatched a burning branch and tied it to Shere Khan's tail. Terrified, the tiger ran away.

Mowgli was very pleased with himself. But he had also realized that perhaps the jungle was a dangerous place for him. It was time to go to the Man-village with Bagheera and Baloo.

The next morning, Mowgli, Baloo, and Bagheera reached the Man-village.

Through the bushes, Mowgli heard a sound he did not know. It was the song of a village girl who had come to the river to fill her water jug.

As he listened to the soft notes of her song, Mowgli felt that he must follow the girl. He crept up the path to the village, drawn by the girl and her song, and followed her through the village gates.

Baloo and Bagheera watched the boy's small figure as long as it could be seen. When Mowgli vanished inside the village gate, Bagheera sighed a deep sigh. He would miss his friend.

Then, with one last look behind them, Baloo and Bagheera headed back into the jungle.